Joey
Goes
to the
Dentist

of related interest

Baj and the Word Launcher
Space Age Asperger Adventures in Communication
Pamela Victor
Cover illustration by Chris Shadoian
ISBN-13: 978 1 84310 830 6   ISBN-10: 1 84310 830 5

Do You Understand Me?
My Life, My Thoughts, My Autism Spectrum Disorder
Sofie Koborg Brøsen
ISBN-13: 978 1 84310 464 3   ISBN-10: 1 84310 464 4

Different Like Me
My Book of Autism Heroes
Jennifer Elder
Illustrations by Marc Thomas and Jennifer Elder
ISBN-13: 978 1 84310 815 3   ISBN-10: 1 84310 815 1

ISPEEK at Home
Over 1300 Visual Communication Images
Janet Dixon
ISBN-13: 978 1 84310 510 7   ISBN-10: 1 84310 510 1

ISPEEK at School
Over 1300 Visual Communication Images
Janet Dixon
ISBN-13: 978 1 84310 511 4   ISBN-10: 1 84310 511 X

Brotherly Feelings
Me, My Emotions, and My Brother with Asperger's
Syndrome
Sam Frender and Robin Schiffmiller
Illustrated by Dennis Dittrich
ISBN-13: 978 1 84310 850 4   ISBN-10: 1 84310 850 X

Personal Hygiene? What's that Got to Do with Me?
Pat Crissey
Illustrated by Noah Crissey
ISBN-13: 978 1 84310 796 5   ISBN-10: 1 84310 796 1

Constipation, Withholding and Your Child
A Family Guide to Soiling and Wetting
Anthony Cohn
ISBN-13: 978 1 84310 491 9   ISBN-10: 1 84310 491 1

Health Care and the Autism Spectrum
A Guide for Health Professionals, Parents and Carers
Alison Morton-Cooper
ISBN-13: 978 1 85302 963 9   ISBN-10: 1 85302 963 7

Yoga for Children with Autism Spectrum Disorders
A Step-by-Step Guide for Parents and Caregivers
Dion E. Betts and Stacey W. Betts
Forewords by Louise Goldberg, Registered Yoga Teacher
and Joshua S. Betts
ISBN-13: 978 1 84310 817 7   ISBN-10: 1 84310 817 8

Joey
Goes
to the
Dentist

By Candace Vittorini
and Sara Boyer-Quick

Featuring Joey Quick

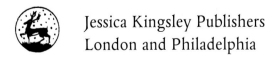
Jessica Kingsley Publishers
London and Philadelphia

With special thanks to the Park Dental Clinic of Coon Rapids, MN

First published in 2007
by Jessica Kingsley Publishers
116 Pentonville Road
London N1 9JB, UK
and
400 Market Street, Suite 400
Philadelphia, PA 19106, USA

www.jkp.com

Library of Congress Cataloging in Publication Data

Vittorini, Candace.
    Joey goes to the dentist / Candace Vittorini and Sara Boyer-Quick.
        p. cm.
    ISBN-13: 978-1-84310-854-2 (hb)
    1. Dentistry--Juvenile literature. 2. Dentists--Juvenile literature. I. Boyer-Quick, Sara. II. Title.
    RK63.V58 2010
    617.6--dc22

                            2006034485

British Library Cataloguing in Publication Data
A CIP catalogue record for this book is available from the British Library

ISBN 978 1 84310 854 2

Printed and bound in the People's Republic of China by Nanjing Amity Printing Co, Ltd
APC-FT4725

Hi! My name is Joey.

I'm 5 years old.

In a couple of days, I am going to the dentist.

I mark it on my calendar so I know when my
appointment is.

Even though I've been there before, some things take me a while to get used to, so I like to practice.

Here we are playing dentist.

My dad counts my teeth just like the dentist does.

I had to get used to the feel
of the toothbrush on my teeth.

When I was little, my mom used a wet washcloth on my gums. Next, I practiced using a toothbrush on my teeth but without toothpaste. The toothbrush felt scratchy on my gums but my teeth couldn't feel the brush. Now I use toothpaste and a toothbrush when I brush my teeth.

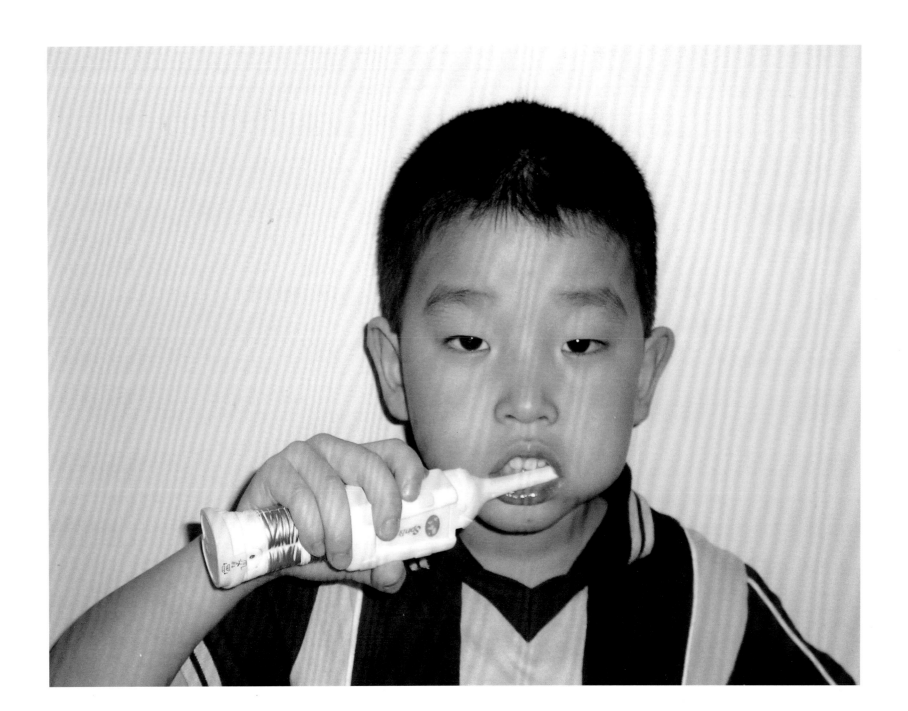

Today is the day of my appointment with the dentist.

Here I am sitting in the waiting room.

When I'm at the dentist's, I usually see both the dentist, Dr Eric Hogan, and the dentist's helper, Jenny. The dentist's helper is a person who really knows a lot about teeth, just like the dentist.

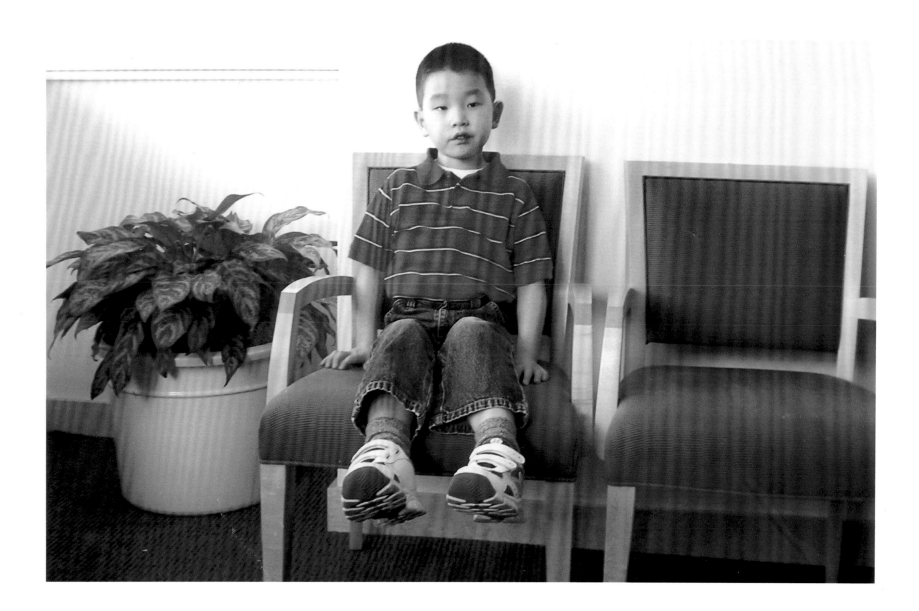

Today, I'm getting X-rays taken.

When I was younger, I used to be a little scared of the X-ray machine. Now I know that X-rays are a type of radiation, which is invisible rays, a bit like Superman's vision. I wear a heavy cover called a lead apron to protect me from the rays. If I'm feeling a bit nervous or worried, sometimes I keep the apron on after the X-rays are over, like a weighted blanket.

Did you know that two thirds of people's teeth are hidden in their gums?

Taking pictures of my teeth helps the dentist make sure that all of my teeth are healthy.

Superman could do that without a machine!

X-rays use film, just like some cameras. The dentist's helper puts a piece of film in my mouth and tells me to bite down on the cardboard part. Sometimes the edges push into my gums a little. This can be uncomfortable, but it only lasts a few seconds.

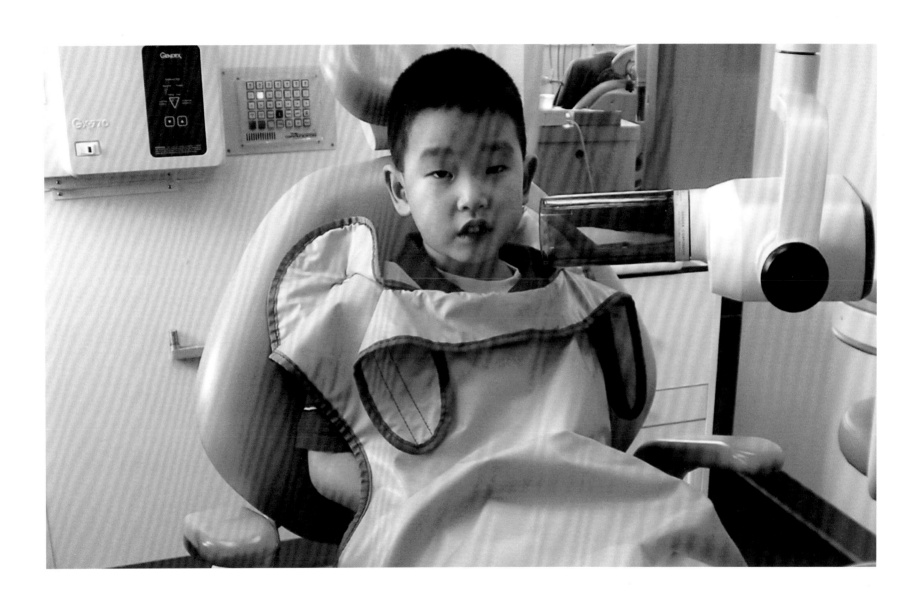

I try to sit very still, so the X-ray machine can get a good picture of my teeth.

When the dentist's helper takes the picture, I hear a little "*Bzz-tt*" sound and then she says, "Open up." I open my mouth and she takes the piece of film. She gives me a new piece of film to bite down on, and takes one more X-ray of a different part of my mouth.

Sometimes I sit there and think about my favorite song, or being a Jedi knight, which helps to take my mind off the cardboard in my mouth.

I'm curious to see what the X-rays of my teeth look like. They develop them right away, so the dentist can have them in just a few minutes.

Here's an X-ray picture of my teeth. What do you think of it?

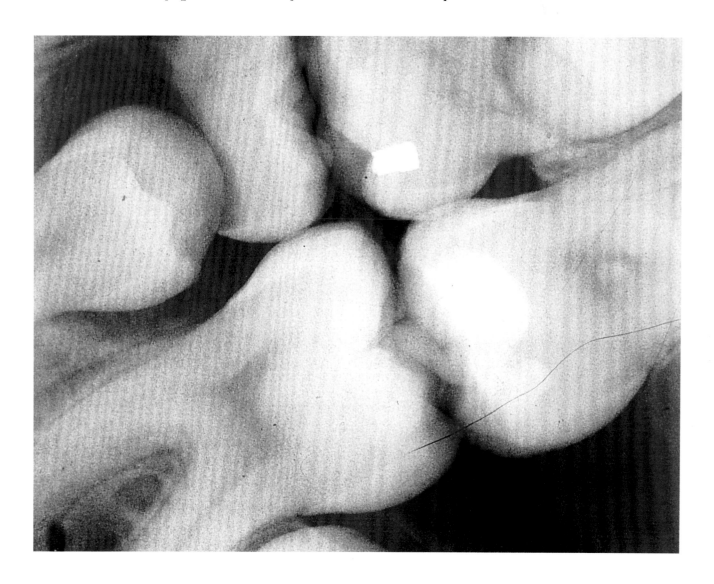

Now my X-rays are all done and I'm feeling okay, so I take the heavy apron off. It's time to sit in the chair and wait for the dentist's helper. I lie back for a minute and think about what my dad and I practiced at home.

When the dentist's helper looks at my teeth,
    I start counting them.
            I think about other things to help me stay calm.

Pretty soon, the dentist's helper comes in and puts a bib over my shirt. Sometimes, when she and the dentist clean my teeth, water and bits of toothpaste spray, so the bib helps keep my shirt clean and dry.

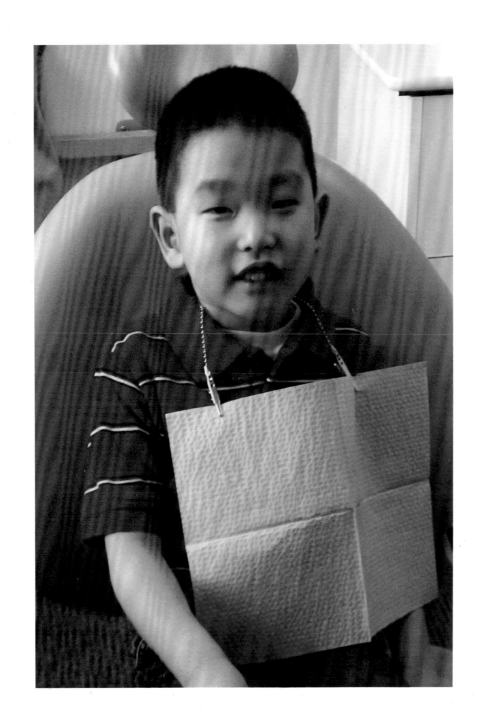

This is a tray with the instruments
that the dentist and dentist's helper
use to look at people's teeth.

The first instrument is a little round mirror. It helps the dentist look at the parts of my mouth that are hard to see. The instrument next to it has a little pointer on the end called an explorer. This makes me think of someone going on a big adventure.

The explorer helps the dentist keep my teeth healthy and strong by removing the built-up layer of old food on my teeth.

Since my teeth are really bones, I usually don't feel any pain, but my teeth and gums feel something vibrating.

When the dentist or dentist's helper leans over me, sometimes the feeling of people being close upsets me. If that happens, I remind myself that it will be over soon, and take some deep breaths.

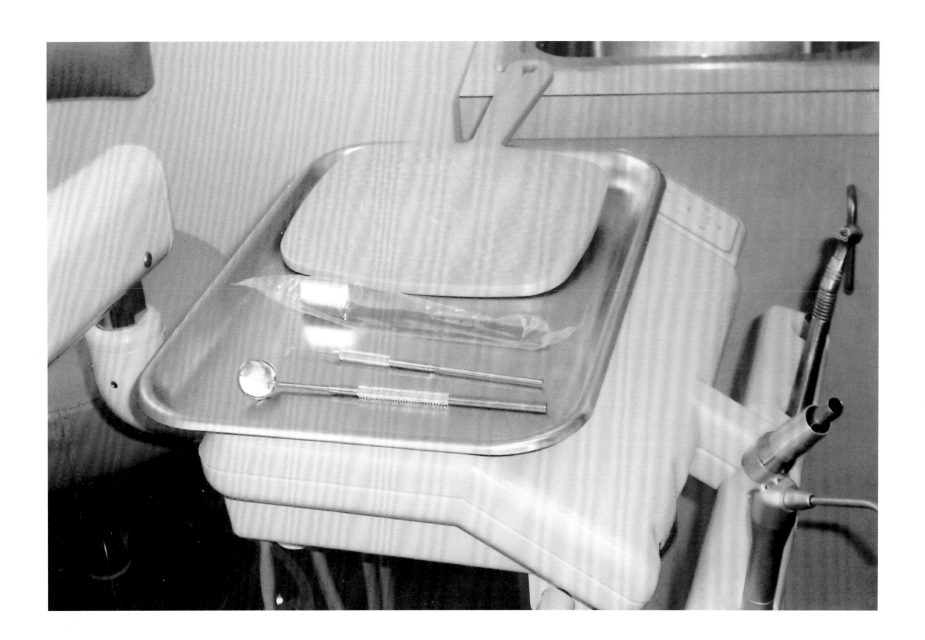

Sometimes, the noises or the smells at the dentist's bother me, so my mom always brings my headphones and my favorite CD to listen to.

Sometimes, she lets me bring my Gameboy™.

Here I am opening wide for my dentist and my dentist's helper. See those masks that they're wearing? It makes them look funny, but the masks protect them from the water that they spray into my mouth and any toothpaste that might be stuck to my teeth.

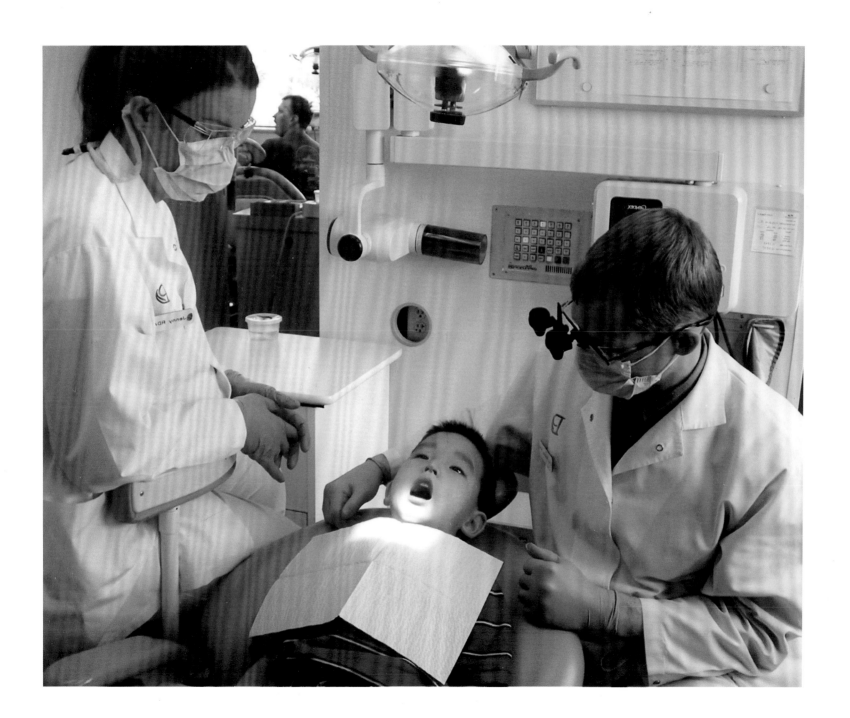

Here's Dr. Hogan looking at my teeth. The light over his glasses reminds me of a spelunker, which is someone who explores caves.

I guess my mouth *is* like a cave, in a way!
While he checks my teeth,
I count to myself and sometimes
I close my eyes for a bit.

After checking my teeth, the dentist's helper puts a type of toothpaste on a little round brush to clean my teeth. As it makes a whirring noise and starts brushing my teeth, I think about going to Burger King™ and getting a Star Wars™ watch and that helps me not to think about the gritty feeling in my mouth. I love Star Wars™ more than anything.

After Jenny's done, she squirts water into my mouth with a tiny hose and sucks it up again. My teeth feel very clean afterwards.

I get used to opening my mouth a lot when I'm here, since everyone wants to see my teeth. That's something Dad and I practiced at home, too.

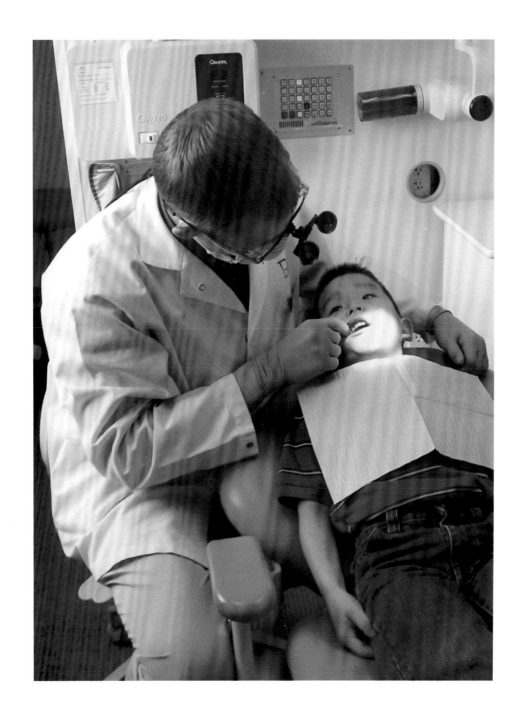

Since we have fluoride in our water where I live, I only need
fluoride treatments once a year.

Fluoride is a gel that helps keep my teeth strong and healthy.

It comes in a tray that looks like a mouth guard.
I like the bubble gum flavor the best. I rub my gums
with my finger before opening my mouth and let my teeth
soak in the trays, as if they're taking a bath.

I remember not to swallow the fluoride,
because it's good for teeth, but not for swallowing.

After two minutes, the dentist takes the tray out.

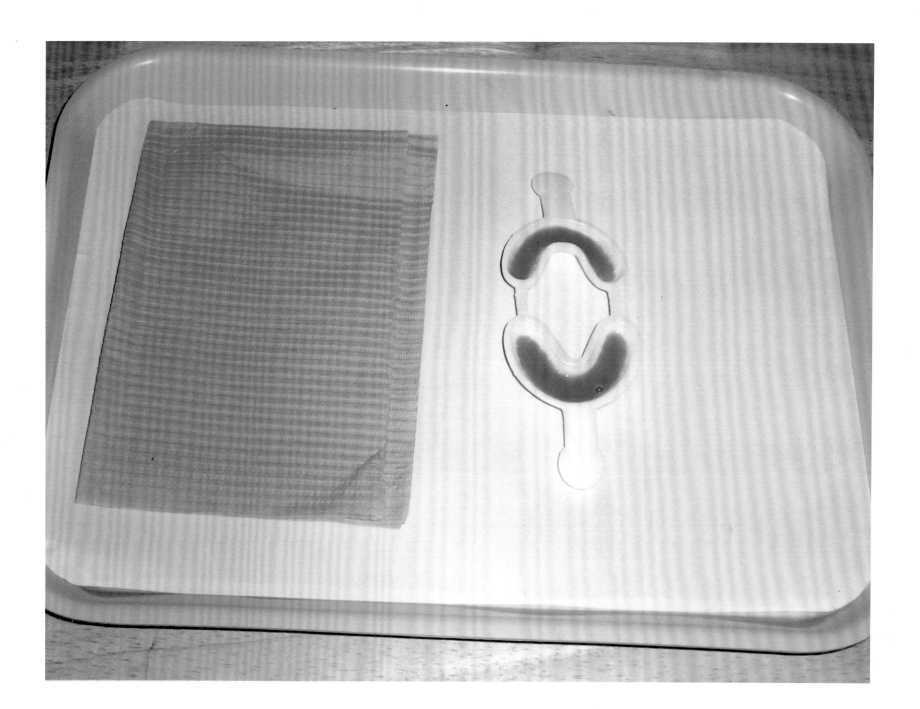

Now I'm all done for today.

My teeth are healthy, and both my dentist and dentist's helper remind me to brush them every day, and not drink too much soda or eat too many sweets. They give me a new toothbrush to take home with me.

Now I can go to Burger King™ and get a new Star Wars™ watch. After that, we'll go home, and I'll show my new watch to my little sister.

I can handle visiting the dentist!

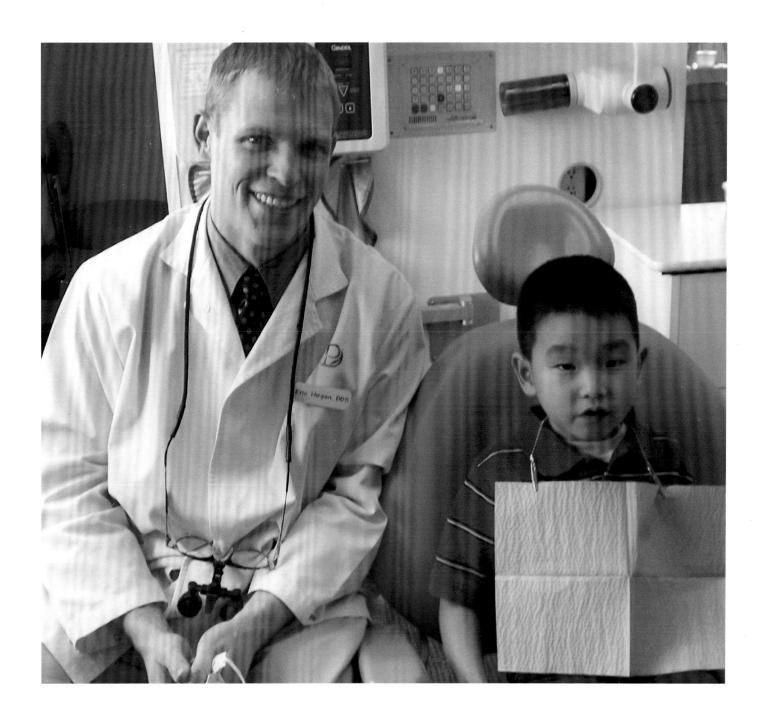

Useful Organizations

International Association for Disability
and Oral Health
www.iadh.org

TEACCH
www.teacch.com

USA

American Association on Health and Disability
110 N. Washington Street, Suite 340
Rockville, MD 20850
Tel: 001 (301) 545 6140
www.aahd.us

American Dental Association
211 East Chicago Avenue
Chicago IL 60611-2678
Tel: 001 (301) 652 2682
www.ada.org

American Occupational Therapy Association
4720 Montgomery Lane
PO Box 31220
Bethesda, MD 20824 1220
Tel: 001 (312) 440 2500
www.aota.org

Autism Society of America
7910 Woodmont Avenue, Suite 300
Bethesda, MD 20814-3067
Tel: 001 (301) 657 0881
www.autism-society.org

Special Care Dentistry Association
401 North Michigan Avenue, Suite 2200
Chicago, IL 60611
Tel: 001 (312) 527 6764
www.scdonline.org

UK

British Association/College of Occupational Therapists
106-114 Borough High Street
London SE1 1LB
Tel: +44 (0)20 7357 6480
www.cot.org.uk

British Dental Association
64 Wimpole Street
London W1G 8YS
Tel: +44 (0)20 7935 0875
www.bda.org

British Society for Disability and Oral Health
138 Woodstock Road
Oxford OX2 7NG
www.bsdh.org.uk

National Autistic Society
393 City Road
London EC1V 1NG
Tel: +44 (0)20 7833 2299
www.nas.org.uk